KAIJU Armageddon

ERIC S BROWN

KAIJU ARMAGEDDON

The USS Flagston was on independent maneuvers in the Atlantic. Captain Neil Green wasn't concerned by the storm raging outside her hull as he lay in his bunk. His crew were well trained at their jobs and the Flagston was one tough ship. Still, despite a long day of inspections, he couldn't sleep. The last few days, he had been more on edge than usual. It wasn't something he could explain. He just had a feeling that *something* was wrong. The feeling made no sense. He had personally made sure the engineers went over every inch of the ship in search of problems that might rear their head when a storm, like the one outside, rolled in.

Though there was trouble in the Middle East, that was usually the case. The United States wasn't openly at war and the Flagston stood a better chance of being hit by a meteor than coming under attack given its current position and route. Truth be told, this mission was nothing more than a shakedown for the new members of her crew and was to iron any hiding wrinkles out of her latest refit.

He stared at the metal ceiling of his cabin, almost wishing the Flagston *was* on duty in the Gulf. At least then, he would know what kind of danger he was up against instead of having to deal with the vague uneasiness that was eating away at him. Cursing himself for being so paranoid, he rolled over onto his side in his rack, and pulled the sheet to cover him higher on his shoulders.

As he finally closed his eyes, his XO's voice came over the internal comm. "Captain Green, we have a situation, sir. Your presence is requested on the bridge."

"What is it?" Captain Green responded.

"This is something you really need to see for yourself, Captain."

Captain Green heard the concern in Lieutenant Commander Baker's tone. Baker had served as his XO for several months now and he knew the man well enough to know that if he was calling, it had to be something important.

Jumping out of bed, Captain Green began to tug on his clothes.

He stumbled out of his quarters, still in the process of shrugging on his shirt and buttoning it as he ran. He passed other members of the crew rushing hurriedly towards their stations.

The XO was calling for him again on the ship wide comm. "Captain to the bridge! Captain to the bridge!"

"I'm on my way," Captain Green grumbled to himself as he picked up his pace. The growing urgency in the XO's now open calls was really beginning to worry him.

****

When Captain Green stepped onto the bridge, the XO, Baker, stood with the ship's radar operator tech, Petty Officer Watson, waiting on him.

"Captain on the bridge!" Lieutenant Herald yelled as he entered and Petty Officer Watson began his report.

"Sir, you need to see this," Watson told him, leading him towards the radarscope. "We've picked up an unidentified surface contact, sir. It's CBDR."

CBDR meant *constant bearing, decreasing range*. Whatever the unidentified surface contact was, it was coming straight at them.

Captain Green looked at the screen of the radarscope.

"What the hades is that?" he asked in disbelief. The surface contact approaching the Flagston was huge. The shape was easily several times that of the Flagston in size.

"We don't know, sir," Watson admitted, "but it's moving at over 30 knots and closing fast."

"That's impossible," Captain Green said, still staring at the radarscope. "Nothing that big can move that fast in the water."

Captain Green could see the surface contact was still a good distance out from the Flagston's position, but at its rate of speed. . .

"It's not answering our hails," the XO added. "Petty Officer Watson here has been studying the contact's movements, sir. He believes it might be a biologic."

Captain Green blinked and stared at Baker as if the XO had lost his mind.

XO Baker shrugged. "We've tried changing course but the surface contact matches us perfectly every time we do."

"Sound general quarters," Neil ordered, "and increase to maximum speed."

"Aye sir! Increasing speed now," the Flagston's helmsman, Seaman Grant shouted.

"Surface contact is matching our speed, sir. Contact in three minutes," Petty Officer Watson warned from his station.

"Giant squid maybe?" the XO half joked, trying to break the tension.

Captain Green shot him a glare.

"Surface contact is increasing speed. It's passing us, sir!"

The Flagston rocked on the waves as something massive tore through the water off her port side. Its wake shook the destroyer as Captain Green saw the top of the thing's giant form through the forward window. It shot by the Flagston as if she were sitting still. A line of armored, triangular shaped fins protruded from the water as it churned about them from the force of the creature's movement.

As the Flagston was jarred about, Captain Green grabbed onto the closet ops station to keep from being knocked to the floor. The bridge was in total chaos. One unlucky yeoman went rolling, clanging into a bulkhead with the sound of bones snapping against metal.

"Enough of this!" Captain Green yelled. "Take unidentified surface contact with guns and blow that thing out of the water."

"Aye, Aye. Taking surface contact with guns," someone told him. "Locked and tracking!"

"Batteries release!" Captain Green barked.

A series of booms followed as the forward guns cut loose. Shells designed to break the back of a battleship rained down on the giant creature.

"Hit Alpha!" someone yelled as explosions flashed in the darkness of the storm. In their light, Captain Green saw the massive monster turn in the water. Its head rose up from the waves. Water rolled off the curves of its thickly scaled, reptilian face. Yellow eyes, each as large a car, glowed with raging fury at the Flagston.

Captain Green could see a purplish, blood like substance leaking from one of the places that shells had struck as the thing outside roared in pain and anger. Captain Green clasped hands over his ears at the sheer intensity of the cry. The hardened glass of the Flagston's windows blew out, sending shards flying like shrapnel across the bridge. The XO took a shard in his forehead and staggered backwards, rivers of red pouring through his hands that had shot up to cover his wound.

The bridge crew was mostly made of veterans, but even so, none of them had ever seen anything like the monster outside before. Panic was growing to a fever pitch and Captain Green knew he had to act quickly.

"Surface contact has altered course and is once again CBDR!"

"Place CIWS in auto!" Neil screamed, trying to keep the fear out of his own voice. The Flagston's close in weapon system sprang to life in a blaze of firepower directed at the *thing* approaching her.

Missiles streaked to meet the creature as shells from the Flagston's main guns rained down on it. Bright tracer rounds from machine gun emplacements slashed the night, cutting into the beast as it closed on the Flagston. The great beast was wailing like a wounded cat but still it came on. It slashed out at the Flagston with a giant hand that was far too human in its shape. Massive claws raked the forward section of the ship, tearing through her armored hull as if it was nothing more than wet paper.

Explosions from within the Flagston herself blossomed in her bowels as the thing's claw struck one of her ordnance lockers.

The lights of the bridge were flicking and small fires had erupted at several of the stations around where Neil held onto the console in front of him for dear life.

The thing outside rose up in the water like a mountain rising up from the waves, and flung itself on top of the Flagston. Its arms wrapped around her sides as metal whined, giving way to the pressure being applied upon it. Then the Flagston was under water.

Captain Neil Green didn't even have time to suck in a breath before it poured over him and washed his feet out from under him. He opened his mouth to scream as salt water flooded his lungs.

****

"What do you mean the Flagston is gone?" Admiral Hutchinson growled at Commander Sigane. "How exactly does one lose a state of the art destroyer?"

Commander Sigane looked pale and on the verge of being sick. "We lost all contact with the Flagston slightly over two hours ago, sir."

Hutchinson grunted, waiting for more information.

"I know what you're thinking, sir. It's more than just tech issues. She's really gone. We've got satellite imaging of what should be her current location and there's. . .well, there's nothing there, sir. It's like the Flagston just disappeared."

Hutchinson's aide, Drew, sat to his right at the table. "Are you suggesting that a hostile took out the Flagston?" Drew asked, leaning forward.

"We don't know what to make it of all, sir," Sigane answered.

"What about the Flagston's transponder?" Hutchinson asked.

Sigane shook his head. "No signal from it, sir. However, it might have been damaged if the Flagston was engaged by a hostile force."

Hutchinson rubbed at his chin with the fingers of his right hand. "Understood. I want all ships in that area on high alert. What's the closest battle group we have to where the Flagston went dark?"

"The Achilles is leading a small task force en route to the Gulf, but even at maximum speed, it would take them half a day to reach the coordinates," Sigane reported.

"Send them," Hutchinson ordered. "We need to know beyond the shadow of a doubt what happened before we go raising too many alarms. I want this kept quiet until we know more."

Sigane nodded.

"The USS Hightown is a part of the Achilles task force, sir," Drew pointed out. "I suggest we have them dispatch some fighters to recon the area ASAP."

"Do it," Hutchinson agreed, "and Drew, get me the president. He needs to know about this."

****

It was a day like any other day on the island of Peaks' Head. Jerry and Raymond drove the winding road down to the beach. The ferry to the mainland was due soon and Jerry couldn't afford to miss it. Summer break was over and he was headed back to college on the mainland. The summer had flown by so fast it seemed as if it hadn't even existed. In no time at all, he'd have his head back in the books and hacking out a thesis paper for his latest degree.

"You could always stay here, ya know?" Raymond spoke up as the jeep they rode in slid around a sharp turn in the road, its wheels spraying gravel. Raymond's style of driving was based on some odd mix of Dukes of Hazard antics and roller coaster stomach churns.

Jerry clutched the armrest next to the rolled down passenger window with a white knuckled grasp. "If you don't slow down, the only place we'll be going is a hospital after you roll this jeep."

Raymond laughed, but if he truly slowed the jeep, Jerry couldn't tell it.

"Just saying I am going to miss you, man. Having you home has been nice."

"Why?" Jerry chuckled, "because dad has something else to be angry over?"

"Well, listening to him yell at you over going off to be a…a. . ."

"Crypto-zoologist," Jerry provided the word.

"Yeah, what you said." Raymond's hand twisted the wheel to take another turn as it came at them. "It's better than listening to him complain about the family business. That's for sure."

Jerry couldn't argue there. The Brysons had always been fishermen. It was like the family curse in some ways as Jerry saw it. Their grandfather had done it, their dad did it, and now Raymond too. Their dad had never forgiven Jerry for not honoring that tradition. The fact that Jerry had worked hard enough in school to earn a full out scholarship and then spent it on something like cryptozoology still rankled the old man. It didn't matter that he had other degrees in more respectable fields as well.

They had hardly spoken over his summer break. Jerry had stayed with Raymond and his wife, Mary Lou, but when their paths *had* crossed, his dad always found an excuse to take off as quickly as he could rather than risk engaging Jerry in the same old disagreement between them. They both knew deep down that neither was ever going to change their mind on their viewpoint of how things should be. Jerry knew he would waste away in a life like his dad and Raymond's and the old man could only see shame in Jerry's chosen career path. It didn't help matters that for the last few years, fishing around Peak's Head was getting to be a rough business. It just wasn't what it used to be. Some, like Jerry's father, blamed the competition while the more liberal folk in the area blamed climate change and pollution. Regardless of the cause, there were fewer and fewer fish to be caught every year.

"Hey bro," Raymond said, tearing Jerry out of his thoughts. He figured Raymond must have seen the mix of emotions playing out in his expression, because he said, "Don't let the old man get to you. I'm proud of you, you know. You're not only the first Bryson who can put the word doctor in front of his name, but you're about to be able to be a doctor twice over."

Raymond pulled the jeep to a stop just short of the docks where the ferry would be arriving. There was a small group of other folks waiting for it. Jerry reached behind him for his bags and tugged them into his lap. "Thanks," Jerry nodded. "That means a lot."

A murmur of excitement spread through the small group waiting for the ferry as Jerry hugged Raymond goodbye and headed for the docks. Jerry walked along the beach, trying to figure out what was going on. Then he saw it. A black, military helicopter was making a beeline for where the group was. It landed just far enough from the docks to be safe and three men spilled out of it. Two of them wore full combat gear and carried nasty looking weapons that Jerry recognized as P-90s from his Stargate fan boy days. The man in the middle wore an expensive suit and dark glasses.

"Dr. Jerry Bryson!" one of the soldiers shouted over the roar of the helicopter blades.

What the… Jerry thought as the trio swept into the ranks of the small group looking for him. He didn't know whether to identify himself or start running after Raymond. His brother was already headed back up the road towards home.

The man in the shades spotted him and started waving at him as he came running over.

"You're Doctor Jerry Bryson, correct?" The man asked.

"That's me," Jerry answered with an edge of reluctance.

"We need you to come with us, sir. There's been an…incident."

****

Space inside the helicopter was cramped. The bird appeared built more for speed and combat than transport. Jerry sat next to the man in the shades as it lifted off and streaked not towards the mainland but out over the open water. The soldiers had given Jerry a headset and the man with the shades and the pilots wore identical ones.

"Look," Jerry said, "you've got the wrong guy. I'm not anyone important."

"I'm special agent Turpin," the man in the shades told him as he began booting up the laptop he'd fished out from underneath his seat. "And I have got something you need to see. Give me just a moment."

Agent Turpin tilted the laptop so Jerry could see the image on its screen. It was a shot of a hole. No, not a hole; it was more like a tunnel. The kind that some burrowing animals made.

Jerry wasn't sure what to make of the image. "What is that? Why do I need to see it?"

"Because, sir, it's 400 feet wide!" Agent Turpin told him, "and it's in Utah."

Jerry still wasn't getting it. Though the two soldiers had their guns resting in their laps and not pointed at him, their presence was making him uncomfortable.

"It's not natural," Agent Turpin explained. "There were earthquakes in the area and in the aftermath, this…whatever it is…was discovered."

"You think you've got a giant gopher on your hands?" Jerry laughed.

Agent Turpin frowned. "No, sir, it is not a gopher, but a giant *something* for sure. We were hoping you could tell us what made it."

"This is joke, right?" Jerry asked.

"Your field of expertise inside of cryptozoology is Kaiju, is it not?"

Jerry nodded very slowly as he looked at the image on the laptop screen again.

"Then you're the man we need, and no, sir, this is *not* a joke."

Jerry felt his breath catch inside him as the aircraft came into view through the window beside where he sat.

"Is that where we're headed?"

Agent Turpin nodded.

Swallowing hard, Jerry tried to hold it together as the helicopter came in for a landing on the carrier's deck. As soon as it touched down, the soldiers and Agent Turpin escorted him into the corridors of the huge ship. They led him to a conference room. A group of very important appearing men and women sat around it.

As Jerry entered the room, two of them got to their feet and moved to greet him. Both of the men were military dress uniforms. Jerry was pretty sure one was a general and the other a very high-ranking naval officer.

"Doctor Bryson, I'm Admiral Hutchinson and this is General Ston. I realize this all very abrupt, but time is of the essence."

"Have a seat, Doctor," the general ordered him, pulling out a chair. "We'll have you up to speed on what's happening in no time."

"Good," Jerry heard himself say, "because I am totally lost."

"Things began a two days ago with the disappearance of the USS Flagston. She was a state of the art destroyer on routine maneuvers. Her disappearance alerted us to the fact that numerous civilian vessels in the Atlantic have recently vanished without a trace as well," Admiral Hutchinson explained.

"But that was just the start," General Ston chimed in. "At nearly the same time the Flagston disappeared, a rash of earthquakes occurred across the entire United States. I'm sure you aware of that if you've been watching the news. . ." Ston paused.

"Don't watch a lot of TV," Jerry replied, "but I'll take your word for it."

"There were a lot of reports pouring in from various areas,

especially Utah that left us scratching our heads. People in the areas where the earthquakes occurred were reporting some pretty strange things. There was talk of monsters and demons rising up from Hell. At first, we didn't know what to make of it all. Then these photos came in," General Ston pointed at screen on the room's far wall.

Jerry exhaled as if someone had just knocked the air out of his lungs as he saw the slide show of images on the screen. "Are those footprints?"

"We believe so," General Ston confirmed.

"Then we found the footage I'm about to show you and we were able to make the connection between the disappearance of the ships and the earthquakes," Admiral Hutchinson said.

The images of the footprints shifted to a real time, badly filmed video that looked as if someone was shooting it from a cell phone. Whoever was filming it seemed to be on a some kind of transport ship in the middle of the ocean. The waters raged around them and it was clear that the person shooting the video was struggling not to be tossed overboard. There was a cacophony of numerous voices crying out in utter terror around the recording device. Its focus moved along the rocking ship, out into the waves. There, in the water, loomed a creature unlike anything Jerry had ever seen in real life. It towered over the ship that the person with the recording device was clinging to. The black scales covering its body gleamed in the last rays of a twilight sun like some kind of armor. The monster's yellow eyes glowed like miniature suns. The thing opened its mouth to show rows upon rows of razor sharp teeth in a roar that was so loud the lens of the recording device cracked and its audio pickups blew out. Jerry flinched as the screen suddenly went black.

"Kaiju," Jerry whispered the word aloud.

"Yes, Doctor Bryson, Kaiju," Admiral Hutchinson said.

"Now are you beginning to understand why you are here?"

****

The rain was pouring from the dark cloud, washing the grime and sand from the car's windshield as Matt sat staring out through it at the crashing waves. Ever since he was a small child, the beach had been his sanctuary. He came here to think and get away. Tonight was no different. His life was in shambles and he was searching for an answer to the trials that were weighing upon him.

Matt had made some bad choices and now he was paying the price. It all started when he took the job at the plant. The promise of higher wages and a better life for his family were too alluring to pass up. Matt just wasn't cut out for the long shifts and overtime that the plant demanded of him though. He had lost the job less than two months after taking it. Beth wasn't working. She wanted to be a stay at home mom for their two children and Matt wanted her to have that.

For the last two days, he faked getting up and heading into work. Sooner rather than later, he would be forced to tell Beth that he had been fired. Their savings were already gone. They'd never had much to begin with and the transmission in Beth's car giving up the ghost wiped it clean.

The only bright spot in all of it was that their house was paid for, thanks to Beth's parents. Her parents had helped them a lot over the years, but even they had nothing left to give. There would be no help coming this time. If anyone was going to save his family and find a way to put food on the table and the bill collectors at bay, it had to be him. Matt, however, didn't have a clue on how he was going to do it.

His hand reached out, turning up the car's heater. Despite it being summertime, the evening rain gave the night air a chill that he felt even inside the car. Autumn was quickly approaching and with it would come higher power bills as their home used electric heat.

Matt's left eye began to twitch from the stress he felt. He rubbed at it, wondering if his health would be the next thing to go south. He turned his attention back to the ocean. As he did, he saw the great beast rising up from the churning waters. It came lumbering towards the shore on legs wider than the car he sat in. His mouth fell open in disbelief. The thing couldn't be real. It stood hundreds of feet tall. Gigantic arms, like those of a man, hung at its sides. An elongated snout protruded from its face. Its eyes burned red like open flames and the ground shook beneath his car as it waded onto the beach.

Matt's bladder released itself. The warmth of his own urine pooled in the driver's seat, soaking his pants. The fear gripping him was so intense that he couldn't even scream. He watched as the monster lifted one of its giant feet and it fell downwards towards him. Then the car's roof was folding inward. The windshield shattered. Shards of glass sprayed over him, burying in his flesh. Before his nerves could fully register the pain though, the monster's foot touched the sand and both he and his car were crushed beneath it.

****

"Sir!" General Ston's aide interrupted the meeting as he burst into the room. "We have landfall!"

Jerry watched as the general and Admiral Hutchinson went pale.

"Where?" General Ston demanded.

"The coast of North Carolina," the aide answered.

The array of screens at the room's far end sprang to life.

Several of them showed panicked reporters shouting and pointing at something in the distance. One screen however showed an aerial view of the monster as it came tearing along the street of a small town. The houses and stores lining the street looked like miniature models in comparison to the beast and the tiny, abandoned cars littering the roadway, the monster stomped along like toys.

"So much for keeping all this quiet," General Ston growled.

"No one knows where the monster came from," one reporter was saying. "Or even what it is. One thing is for sure, though, it's hostile and royally ticked off."

Another reporter was screaming, "The government has issued an evacuation order for all towns north of Sedgewig. I repeat, if you are in any of those areas, leave now. The National Guard is being mobilized in an attempt to stop the creature but. . ."

The aerial shot of the creature was being filmed by a rather brave or stupid reporter and his crew aboard a network helicopter. The monster's face grew larger on that screen as the helicopter drew closer to it. One of the thing's enormous hands lashed out. Jerry saw the flash of its claws before the screen went black.

On another screen, Jerry saw the helicopter, or what was left of it, spinning through the air. Black smoke rolled from the falling bird before it struck the top in a fiery crash of what looked to be a hospital.

"Scramble everything we have in that area!" Admiral Hutchinson was yelling at his staff. "I don't care who the acting officer over that region is! Do it on my authority!"

"My boys are already responding," General Ston told Jerry, motioning at the screens.

A trio of tanks was rolling down the street into the path of the giant creature. Their main guns were raising upwards to target it. Behind them, a convoy of transport trucks and APCs were deploying troops in a firing line almost a quarter of mile back.

The tanks opened fire. The first round impacted with the creature's stomach in an explosion of orange and yellow flames. The second and third shots struck its legs and hips with equal force as the monster roared in pain and fury. Jerry could see that the rounds had done damage to the Kaiju. A purplish goo leaked from its mangled flesh at the points of their contact. The monster leaned over and with one sweep of its claws, reduced one tank to a wreck of shredded and crushed metal while sending another bouncing across the street into the front of a gas station. Sparks flew each time the tank clanged against the pavement until it tore through the station's row of pumps and ignited the gasoline that sprayed from them. The station and tank were engulfed by a blast of heat and light that stretched upwards into the early morning sky.

The sole surviving tank was trying to turn and run as the Kaiju lowered one of its feet onto the armored vehicle and it too exploded as its own ordnance detonated. The Kaiju yanked its foot away from the burning wreckage of the tank with a shriek of pain.

At that moment, the firing line of infantry and APCs opened up on the great beast. The cacophony of small arms fire was deafening.

"Somebody turn that down!" General Ston shouted.

Shoulder braced RPGs let loose amid the chaos. The Kaiju didn't stagger from the assault. It leaped forward, charging the mass of soldiers. Men screamed and died as it plowed through them and towered above their position. The ranks of soldiers broke with men and women fleeing in any direction they could.

"Sweet Christmas," Jerry heard General Ston whisper. Then louder, he shouted, "Have them fall back! Now!"

A group of F-16 came roaring in. Missiles flew from their wings, striking the Kaiju's head and shoulders. The great beast reeled and spun about to face them as they continued on towards it. The forward guns of the fighters blazed, spewing high velocity, armor piercing rounds into its face and throat. The fighters sped past the monster and came about for another run at it.

One of the Kaiju's hands plunged downward, snatching up an overturned eighteen-wheeler from the ground. The cab of the vehicle snapped loose from the trailer as the Kaiju lifted it. The Kaiju swung the trailer like a baseball bat at the approaching cluster of fighters. Two of the F-16s were caught in its arc. They erupted like fireworks, raining flaming debris into the surrounding town below. The Kaiju flung the remains of the trailer away and jumped to meet a third fighter as it tried to pass by. One of the monster's hands caught hold of the fighter, pulling it close. The fighter and Kaiju exploded as the beast hugged the F-16 to its chest.

When the smoke cleared, the Kaiju was still standing, if barely. Its chest was a mass of mangled and charred tissue. It swayed like a boxer trying desperately not to collapse. The remaining two F-16s took advantage of its pause and came barreling in once more, hitting it with everything they had. The Kaiju whined as it tried to reach out for them, but this time the fighters were too fast for it in its injured state.

"Fall, damn you," Admiral Hutchinson said from where he stood only a few feet from Jerry's seat.

Another network helicopter had appeared on the scene.

"Get that bird out of there!" General Ston was screaming.

The Kaiju gave a roar and began to run, its huge feet leaving giant imprints in the street as it continued on for the edge of the town. By pure accident, the network helicopter found itself in the monster's path. The Kaiju slammed into the helicopter at full out run. The helicopter exploded like a landmine against the Kaiju's wounded flesh, its blades slashing at the monster like swords before they were reduced to pieces of broken metal. The pieces that didn't bury themselves in the Kaiju's flesh, spun away before clattering to the street.

The Kaiju was a smoking and bleeding mess as dropped to its knees and finally collapsed, face first, on top of the roof of a department store. The building splintered and folded inward from its weight.

A cheer rang out from the others in the room around Jerry, but he didn't join them. His gut told him this was just the opening battle in a new war that would forever change the world, as humanity knew it.

****

"Whatever you need." Those were powerful words when they came from someone of the rank that Admiral Hutchinson possessed and the admiral had the power of the president behind him.

Jerry took full advantage of it. The fallen Kaiju was the greatest gift to the science of cryptozoology since its birth. The aircraft carrier he'd original been summoned to wasn't far from where the Kaiju made landfall. He was en route to the site aboard the fastest bird the carrier had at its disposal. Supposedly, all the equipment he asked for would be waiting for him upon his arrival or arriving very shortly thereafter.

The towns around the site remained evacuated and the military had sealed off the entire area where the battle had taken place. When the copter carrying him touched down, Jerry hit the ground running. The Admiral had a staff waiting for him as well. Some were scientists from the various fields that Jerry thought he might need at his disposal and the rest were doctors and containment teams drafted from the CDC in Atlanta.

He supposed the CDC teams were a blessing. If there was a biological hazard carried by the Kaiju, they would be equipped to deal with it. Otherwise, the medical staff was useless beyond running base general base tests on the tissue samples Jerry ordered harvested.

The next two days were a whirlwind of data gathering and study. Admiral Hutchinson and General Ston checked in with him constantly, eager for him to find something out about the exotic and destructive creature that had just waded out of the ocean and into North Carolina.

Jerry kept an eye on the news while he worked, trying to pick up on anything unusual that could be a sign of more Kaiju. Both General Ston and the admiral were well aware that the creature was not the only one of its kind. The cell phone footage Jerry had been shown upon his arrival on the carrier alone confirmed that. The beast showed it was not the same one the military had just, at great cost, put down.

At the end of his second day, Jerry was torn away from his study of the fallen beast and whisked back to stand before the general and admiral once more. The soldiers they sent to collect him had ignored his pleas for more time. There was still so much to learn from the Kaiju's corpse.

The soldiers who escorted him into the room aboard the carrier where the Ston and Hutchinson waited took their places near the door as Jerry took his seat at the table in the center of the room.

General Ston leaned forward in his seat. "Well?"

Jerry plopped folders stuffed to overflowing with papers onto the table. "I can tell you it is indeed a Kaiju and there are certainly more of them."

"Tell us something we don't know," Admiral Hutchinson demanded.

"This one was a child," Jerry said.

"Excuse me?" General Ston bellowed.

"You heard him," Admiral Hutchinson told the general, silencing the older man so Jerry could continue.

"Samples of supposed Kaiju tissues from around the globe were shipped in for me to compare to the tissue and DNA from this one. As one would think, most of them were fakes, but not all. From the handful of other legitimate samples at my disposal, I was able to establish a rough baseline. You see, though this Kaiju is the first to be *known* to exist, sightings of the great beasts go back as far as feudal Japan and before."

"Thank you, Dr. Bryson. Please continue," Admiral Hutchinson urged.

Jerry cleared his throat. "I believe there has been some kind of *event* on the ocean floor. Whatever has happened has awakened the Kaiju. Many cryptozoologists have speculated that the creatures have been asleep on the ocean floor and in its trenches for centuries. Now that they are awake, it's a certainty that we will be seeing more of them. This Kaiju coming onto land will not be an isolated incident. I believe the Kaiju will rise in en mass and seek to regain dominance of the planet."

"Regain?" Admiral Hutchinson asked.

"Yes," Jerry nodded. "Current Kaiju theory suggests that once, long before man, maybe even before the dinosaurs, this planet belonged to them."

General Ston laughed and shot the admiral an annoyed look.

"This is ludicrous. Where do you find freaks like this?" He stabbed at thumb at Jerry.

"Dr. Bryson is one of the leading experts in his field," the admiral said, his voice calm and cold. "Up until a week ago, General, none of us truly believed things like the Kaiju existed. Two days ago, our forces engaged one. I'd say it's time for a little out of the box thinking, wouldn't you?"

General Ston grunted. "What does it matter what they are or where they came from? We need to know how many there are and where they're likely to strike next. We can't afford to keep getting caught with our pants down."

Jerry's head jerked around towards the general. "What? Has there been another attack?"

"Two actually," Admiral Hutchinson informed him. "A Kaiju attacked an oil rig off the coast of New Orleans and another came ashore in China. We were able to keep both incidents out of the media this time for the most part with the help of Chinese government."

"Three attacks in less than the same number of days," Jerry said aloud as he ran his fingers through his hair. "Will I have access to the bodies?"

"No. I am afraid not," Admiral Hutchinson informed him. "The attack on the oil rig was a hit and run. That Kaiju was long gone before a proper response could be mounted. The one in China disappeared back into the ocean, as well, after a prolonged battle with the Chinese military who were unable to stop it."

"I see," Jerry frowned.

"Doctor," Admiral Hutchinson frowned as well. "I am sure you understand how pressed for time we are. Is there *anything* can tell us that may prove useful against these Kaiju?"

"I can't predict when or where the ocean-based Kaiju will strike if that's what you're asking," Jerry shrugged. "I can't tell you how many there are either, but I would guess their number is at best in the hundreds."

"Hundreds? And the one we stopped was a child?" Admiral Hutchinson raised a hand to his face, massaging his cheeks with its fingers.

"Do you have any idea how much damage a hundred of those things could do, son?" General Ston asked.

"That said," Jerry continued, unfazed, "I can tell you a lot more about the Kaiju inside the borders of the United States."

Both General Ston and the admiral sat up straighter in their chairs.

"I didn't have much time to examine the data you provided me with on the incident in Utah, but I can confirm that the burrow you discovered after the quakes is indeed Kaiju in origin. As I am sure you've already concluded, that Kaiju *was* the cause of the earthquakes. I have a team attempting to track its movements, as we speak, via seismographs. Currently, the creature is so deep underground that getting a clear reading on it is difficult but I believe that ultimately, we will be able to provide you with an approximation of where it will surface." Jerry grinned. "That one, at least, you can be ready for."

Admiral Hutchinson stared at him. "Anything else, Doctor? Anything at all?"

"No two Kaiju are going to be alike. Though, according to current theory, all Kaiju share a baseline reptilian DNA, each one will have its own strengths and weakness depending on what other animal, or blend there of, animal characteristics the given Kaiju possesses."

"Understood," Admiral Hutchinson rose from the table. "Thank you, Dr. Bryson. That will be all...for now."

****

Dr. Bryson's team estimated the arrival of the burrowing Kaiju in the city of New York at 9 AM eastern standard time. The city was in the last stages of evacuation and under martial law as the military prepared to intercept the beast. Columns of tanks rolled along empty streets and there were numerous mobile command units scattered around New York. A pair of Apaches flew by overhead as Jerry stepped out of his team's own mobile headquarters. It was basically an armored lab on wheels on loan from the military. The vehicle had originally been designed for nuclear disposal/HAZMAT purposes, but now its interior resembled something more like the CDC would use.

Jerry had demanded to be present for the Kaiju's arrival. He wanted to see a live specimen up close and personal. Two heavily armed APCS served as escort to his mobile lab. His being here was a risk that Admiral Hutchinson wasn't comfortable with. Jerry knew there were plenty of other cryptozoologists that could be called in should something happen to him but it would take time to bring them up to speed and time was a precious commodity given the circumstances.

So far, his team had been unable to pinpoint the exact location that the Kaiju would emerge from, but Jerry hoped that as it neared the surface, that would change. No one had ever tracked a Kaiju so deep under the Earth's crust before and most of his gear for doing so was cobbled together from basic geology equipment, refitted to serve that purpose.

He stood staring up at a random office building, thinking about how fragile the world of man really was. The amount of devastation a single Kaiju could do in a city like New York was staggering.

"Dr. Bryson!" Anna shouted as she came bounding out of the mobile lab towards him. "We've lost the Kaiju!"

Jerry spun around. "What? How?"

"The Kaiju's speed spiked. One minute, it was approaching from the west, and the next, it was just…gone."

Jerry shoved Anna aside, racing for the lab to check the equipment's reading himself. He made it three steps before he realized it was too late. The ground shook beneath him and he knew it was tremors produced from the Kaiju surfacing.

A deafening roar rang out in the distance followed by the sound of heavy weapons being fired en mass.

****

A 300-foot section of the street simply gave way taking a skyscraper with it. The tall building, with its foundation gone, tumbled over in a shattering mass of debris. Colonel Stephens was in command of the defenses allotted to the area. One of the four tanks on the street had been lost as the hole formed, falling downwards into its darkness. The others backed away from the hole as their main guns pivoted to come to bear on it. Colonel Stephens thanked God that the infantry division under his command had been out of range of the skyscraper as it fell or the street would already be slicked with the blood of dead and dying men.

He'd been briefed on the nature of the Kaiju, but as the great beast surfaced and he saw it with his own eyes, it was all he could do to stand his ground. It exploded upwards out of the hole. Even with half its body still underground, the thing towered two hundred feet above him. The creature appeared to be a strange cross between an earthworm, a centipede, and an armadillo. Numerous short, burly arms protruded from its worm shaped central mass ending in claws larger than a fully-grown man. Its head was a pointy, snouted bump at the top of its body. Four sets of insect-like eyes ran in the pattern of an upside down J along the sides of its skull. A pair of mandibles snapped open and closed over what appeared to be a circular mouth in the center of the Kaiju's face. Though its central mass was shaped like a worm's, that was the only resemblance. The creature's body was covered in thick armored plates that overlay each other along its length.

"Fire!" Colonel Stephens screamed. "All units, fire at will!"

The main guns of tanks boomed over the crackle of small arms fire as sniper teams opened up with RPGs from nearby windows. Shells and rockets exploded as they collided with the Kaiju's armored form, the flashes of explosions blossoming and fading like Christmas tree lights all over the Kaiju's central mass. The creature swayed like a snake, deciding where to strike, as Colonel Stephens' men kept up their rate of fire.

The Kaiju flopped onto the street, lowering itself onto its arms, legs, whichever they were, to crawl from the hole like a centipede. It tore through the line of tanks, crushing them as it moved over them. Its body was so huge that it scraped away entire sections of the buildings lining the street as it moved forward. Some of the buildings toppled on top of the monster but it ignored them as their debris bounced as harmlessly off its armored form as all the firepower the colonel's men were throwing at it.

In less than two minutes, half of the colonel's command was dead, trampled or buried under rubble from the collapsing buildings

"Fall back!" Colonel Stephens was yelling as the Kaiju continued forward on a direct path for the APC he sat in the turret of. His hands found the fire controls of the mounted machine gun in front of him and he leveled it at the Kaiju's head. Tracer rounds glowed hot as they flew at the monster. Sparks flew as the bullets pinged away and ricocheted off the creature's skull.

The APC's driver had kicked the vehicle into reverse and its engine strained to move out of the raging Kaiju's path. The monster was too fast. It barreled into the APC, knocking it aside as the foot of a running child would a toy left upon a bedroom floor. The APC was hurled sideways, into the air, before it smashed through and into the second floor of an office building. Colonel Stephens' exposed portion of his upper body was ripped away from his lower half in the process.

****

"Alpha One Bravo coming into range," Captain Hawkins said into the mic that dangled from the lower portion of his pilot helmet as he brought his Apache in for a strafing run. The Kaiju was moving somewhere in the neighborhood of forty miles per hour through the streets of New York, leaving a trail of destruction in its wake. Alpha Two Bravo was accompanying him on the run. The two Apaches were spaced out but coming in hot from the same vector.

Captain Hawkins emptied every launcher aboard his Apache in a single volley as Alpha Two Bravo's pilot followed suit. Missiles streaked earthwards, lighting up the Kaiju's back with flashes of orange and yellow. The two Apaches slowed, waiting on the smoke to clear. Captain Hawkins screamed, jerking his Apache hard to the right, as the Kaiju's head came through the smoke at him. The giant beast had shifted its body so that its upper half wound around into the air to strike at the helicopters. Captain Hawkins watched Alpha Two Bravo disappear in a burst of blazing flames as the Kaiju's mandibles sunk into its sides.

In his haste to avoid the Kaiju's attack, Captain Hawkins had forgotten the theater in which he was engaged. Alpha One Bravo veered into the side of a building. Its blades broke against the metal and bricks they made contact with there. He had just enough time for a final scream before his Apache struck the building full on and exploded around him.

****

Jerry's heart froze in his chest as he saw the Kaiju go skittering pass the end of the street where his team's mobile lab was parked. He could see its massive form between two buildings in the distance, and despite its increasing speed, the thing's body seemed to stretch on forever before it finally disappeared from sight.

"Holy mother…" he heard Anna mutter beside him. "They're not going to be able to stop that thing, are they?"

Jerry didn't have an answer. Not one he wanted to say aloud anyway. He darted into the mobile lab and hurried to get General Ston on the line.

"What the hell do you want, Dr. Bryson?" General Ston roared when Jerry finally got through to him. "I'm kind of busy right now!"

"I know how to stop this thing!" Jerry shouted. "You have to force it into the water and keep it there! That's the only thing that's going to work!"

"Drown it?" General Ston growled the question.

"Exactly!" Jerry answered. "New York is an island! Just get it into the water!"

"Get me satellite imaging of the battle now!" Jerry ordered his staff as the general broke communication.

Jerry watched as the forces deployed in New York repositioned themselves around the creature. Tanks had been rendered useless by the Kaiju's speed. They simply couldn't keep up with it. All hope rested with the fighters and helicopters that had been brought in for the city's defense. If they could just herd the thing into the water, all this would be over as quickly as it started. Jerry was banking on the fact that creature breathed like a worm despite its armor.

Dozens of Apaches were giving chase, firing everything they had as squadrons of various fighters came in tearing in ahead of the Kaiju, emptying their payloads in an effort to drive the creature eastward. No matter how powerful the Kaiju might be, it lacked intelligence, shifting its course each time the fighters intercepted it.

As it reached the shoreline, General Ston's forces made a concentrated strike against it, driving it on, and into the water. The great beast splashed in, moving at close to fifty-five miles an hour. It tried to twist its body around and cling to the shore, but the onslaught of missiles and directed bombs were too much for it. Their impacts kept it from coming about and it went sprawling into the depths, carried on by its own momentum.

The great beast sank like a rock, its arm-like legs flailing. The water churned and bubbled violently above it as the Apaches and other attack birds moved in to keep it pinned down. The battle lasted five minutes that crept by like an eternity, before the waters became calm and there was no sign of the Kaiju.

Jerry let out a sigh of relief as he crumbled into one of the mobile lab chairs and the battle was finally over.

****

The bulk of New York Island resembled a post-apocalyptic wasteland. General Ston's troops were attempting to regroup and salvage what they could. One thing was clear though, the military couldn't keep on at this rate. In a war of attrition, the Kaiju would surely win. It took hundreds if not thousands of lives and countless millions in equipment costs to stop a single one of the great beasts.

Already, there had been over a dozen Kaiju attacks in other

nations and none of them had fared as well as the United States thus far. By all accounts, London was merely gone. Hundreds of miles of South America were ravaged by the Kaiju. The Russians had resorted to the use of their nuclear arsenal and the Ukraine would be glowing in the dark for decades to come. Even now, Australia was engaged in a losing conflict against a group of Kaiju that had come ashore there. Things were looking pretty bleak for the continued existence of the human race.

Jerry switched off the TV in the apartment he had been assigned as his temporary quarters as a knock sounded on his door. He got up and went to answer it. Admiral Hutchinson, accompanied by two armed soldiers, was waiting in the hallway.

"The president wants to see you, Dr. Bryson," the admiral told him. "You'll be flying out for DC within the hour. I suggest you gather up anything you need."

"*You* came to tell me that in person, sir?" Jerry asked.

Admiral Hutchinson laughed, though his laughter was strained.

"No, son, I came to talk with you before you left." The Admiral stepped into the apartment, motioning for the two soldiers to stay outside. He shut the door and moved to take a seat on the couch.

Jerry followed him.

"The Russians deployed nukes against the Kaiju at 16 hours, our time."

"I heard," Jerry said. "It's all over the news."

"Didn't do them a lot of good. Sure, they took out five of the Kaiju based on the reports I've seen but the cost. . ."

"I know," Jerry agreed.

"I got you involved in all of this, Dr. Bryson, because I believed you could find an answer to stopping these monsters." Admiral Hutchinson met his eyes. "I need you to be straight with me now, son. Can you do that or is this the end of the world?"

"I don't know," Jerry answered honestly.

"Well, I hope you can, because if you can't, we're all well and truly FUBARed."

They stared at each other in silence for a moment before the admiral spoke again.

"The president will want to use nukes too, now that the Russians have opened that playing field."

"You and I both know that won't work," Jerry agreed. "We'll just be helping the Kaiju destroy our world if we do. Besides, based on what I have learned about the Kaiju, only the main blast of a nuke will harm them. The radiation won't so much as faze most of them. It might even mutate them into something worse than we're already dealing with."

"Tell him that, Jerry. Make *sure* he understands," the admiral ordered, and then he got up and left without another word, leaving Jerry staring after him.

****

Dr. Jerry Bryson never imagined he would be standing in front the President of the United States and his cabinet giving a report, but here he was. His throat was dry and it was all he could do to stop his hands from shaking.

"Dr. Bryson," President Gregory said, "I understand you're the best expert we have on these. . ."

"Kaiju," Jerry filled in the blank.

"The military is telling me that this an apocalyptic level event. Is that true, Doctor?"

"It depends on how you define that, sir. The Kaiju will set us back to the Stone Age, so to speak, but I find it highly unlikely they will exterminate all human life on the planet. There are simply too few of them."

"I am told that you advise against the use of tactical nuclear weapons."

"Yes sir. In the current situation, it is my belief that they will do more harm than good. Only the direct blast of a detonating nuke will harm or kill a Kaiju. The radiation of such weapons of mass destructing yield though will make life very difficult for us and weaken our position against them. As the Kaiju continue to come onto land, we will need to defend our industries and farms at all costs, not drop bombs on them."

"The Russians were able to kill multiple Kaiju with a single nuclear strike, Doctor. Yes, they have written off part of their country to kill them, but according your own reports, the Kaiju at best likely only number in the hundreds, perhaps less."

"And perhaps more, sir. I have no hard data to backup my assumption that there numbers is that finite. As large as the Kaiju are, it stands to reason however that their numbers would be limited by nature herself."

"So you're saying these things aren't alien in nature or mutations, but they are a natural occurrence?"

"Very little is known about the Kaiju, Mr. President. Up until our war with them began, they were only legends. I have teams scattered across the globe, working to learn more in conjunction with my teams inside the United States, but. . ." Jerry paused, searching for the correct words. "We're starting from basically a zero point and going forward from there."

"If we do not resort to nuclear strikes, what do you suggest we do, Dr. Bryson? It's clear that as powerful as this country's military is, they are not up to dealing with a threat of this level."

Jerry was sweating. He fidgeted nervously on his feet, unable to stop himself from doing so.

"Do you have a solution, Doctor?" President Gregory asked.

"Given time, my staff and I might be able to come up with a biological weapon that would be effective against the Kaiju."

There. I've said it. Jerry thought. He was a firm believer that such things were unthinkable but there appeared to be no other choice.

"Time is not something we have a lot of right now, Doctor. The number of Kaiju coming ashore is increasing with each passing day."

"All Kaiju share a baseline DNA, Mr. President. It's only a matter of finding something that effects them and not us."

Jerry was stalling for time more than for anything else. In truth, he had no idea if such a weapon could be manufactured fast enough to deal with the Kaiju threat. Science was not something that happened overnight, but he couldn't live with himself he didn't try everything possible in keeping the president from nuking American citizens in an attempt to stop the monsters. No matter how much effort was put into evacuations, there would always be someone who stayed. Combining that with the unpredictable appearances of the Kaiju, and the use of nuclear weapons was as much a death sentence for America as the monsters themselves were.

"You have two days, Doctor," President Gregory told him. "That said, I will not completely rule out the use of nuclear strikes should the Kaiju come at us en mass before those two days are up."

"Thank you, Mr. President," Jerry said and fled the room as fast as his legs would carry him.

Jerry was rushed aboard the fastest jet available and flown back to New York where his core team, who had been with him since his first day on the job as the US Kaiju expert, awaited him.

****

"Captain on the bridge!" the XO barked as he entered.

Captain Page was in a foul mood. "Coffee," he snarled at a yeoman who ran to fetch him a cup. The crew of the Allentown was long over due a shore leave and he missed his family. His little girl was turning three tomorrow, and once again, he was going to miss her birthday.

"Report," Captain Page ordered.

"All quiet, sir," the XO answered.

The Allentown was a nuclear submarine. Like most of the other vessels of her class, she'd been tasked with standing watch for Kaiju movements, maneuvering up and down the eastern coastline of the US. Thus far, things in her sector had remained calm and without incident but Captain Page knew things could change at the drop of a dime. It was easy for crews to grow bored and careless on missions like this one. That was part of the reason he rode the crew so hard. Normally, a crew feared the EX more than the captain, but not aboard the Allentown.

The yeoman returned with his coffee, handing it to him.

Captain Page sipped at it as he looked around at the officers on duty. They all appeared as tired as he felt. An air of tension hung over them. The Kaiju had everyone on edge. There was talk of the rise of the Kaiju signaling the end of the human race. Captain Page didn't know how he felt about that. It was difficult to believe the very existence of mankind was threatened by the creatures. Yes, they were powerful and gigantic, but at the end of the day, the Kaiju were merely a new breed of animal that had finally been discovered.

"Contact to port!" Petty Officer Weaver shouted and went pale as he added, "Multiple contacts! CBDR sir!"

"Kaiju?" the XO asked.

"What else could they be?" Captain Page's coffee sloshed over the sides of his cup as he rushed to stand behind Weaver and look over the man's shoulder at the data on the screen. For the first time in years, cold fear clawed at Captain Page's gut as he counted the number of contacts. There were over two dozen of them, moving at over 40 knots.

"Impact in two minutes, sir," Petty Officer Weaver warned him.

"Engines to full! Hard to starboard!" Captain Page ordered.

"Aye sir!" Seaman Falker responded from the Allentown's helm.

"Get Naval Command on the line and inform that the Allentown is engaging a large group of hostile contacts at our current position!" Captain Page knew deep down in that moment that he wouldn't be going home to see his little girl again. "Guns, take the lead contact. Hit that bastard with all forward tubes!"

A volley of torpedoes rocketed out of the Allentown. They sped through the water toward their target as the Allentown's bridge crew counted the seconds until impact.

"Hit Alpha!" Petty Officer Weaver announced.

"Status of contact?" Captain Page demanded.

"Still closing fast, sir!   Speed increasing to 50 knots!"

Outside the hull of the Allentown, a Kaiju swam towards the sub like a guided missile. Numerous other Kaiju followed in its wake. The lead Kaiju had no arms. Instead, its upper body resembled that of a squid. Tentacles whipped about in the water, propelling it forward at an impossible speed. The tip of its pointed head was aimed at the middle of the Allentown. It plowed into the submarine with enough force to break the Allentown in half. The two pieces of the broken sub drifted apart in the water as the other Kaiju adjusted their course to swim over them as they sank.

****

Admiral Hutchinson read over the report, his eyes growing wide. The largest group of Kaiju ever encountered to date was en route for the coast of South Carolina. The original report had come in from the Allentown and all contact with the sub was lost shortly thereafter. He had known Captain Page and the loss of such a good man saddened him. There was no time to mourn though. A group of Kaiju that size was very likely to prove unstoppable. They would likely bowl over everything the US could throw into their path and just keep coming. Of course, that didn't mean it wasn't his duty to try.

General Ston was already busy coordinating the deployment of his forces at the point where the Kaiju would be coming ashore. Everything from trains to transport planes was being used to scramble men and equipment to that location. The Navy had no ships within range to reach the point of arrival of the pack of Kaiju in time. Admiral Hutchinson had hedged his bets that the Kaiju would continue with their more northern-based assault on the US and now he was paying the price for it. It was going to be up to his counterpart, Admiral Worley in the Air Force to provide support for General Ston's massing defenses.

Admiral Hutchinson fished his cell out of the pocket of his uniform pants.

"Admiral," Dr. Jerry Bryson answered, sounded surprised. "I wasn't expecting to hear from you so soon."

"Tell me your weapon is ready, Doctor. We've got the largest group of Kaiju on record coming ashore in South Carolina within the hour."

There was a pause before the doctor answered. "We have a prototype, Admiral. It's a virus that we believe to be effective. The virus will attached itself to the baseline Kaiju DNA and attack it, acting like a fast moving cancer. It's untested, of course."

"How fast acting?" Admiral Hutchinson asked.

"It depends on the Kaiju. As you know, they're all different by varying degrees."

"I need more than that."

"Best case? The virus could result in death within minutes of exposure to it. Worst case, it won't work at all." Dr. Bryson paused. "But, Admiral, there is something else to keep in mind. This virus was designed in a matter of days. I can't guarantee that it will be harmless to us."

"That's a chance we'll have to take, Doctor," the admiral sighed. "There are over two dozen Kaiju in this pack. If your virus doesn't work, those monsters won't be stopping in South Carolina. They'll rampage their way right into the heart of the US and keep on going."

"I need more time," Dr. Bryson suddenly pleaded. "This virus. . ."

"I'm sorry, Doctor. I want every ounce of the virus you've cooked up so far en route to South Carolina right now. Time is one thing that we no longer have any left of."

****

General Ston had done enough of sitting in a safe, far distant war room, watching men die. Today, he stood atop the hill that overlooked the beach where his forces were deploying. Columns of tanks came streaming up the sand to fan out and form a double-layered firing line facing the ocean. Behind them sat various mobile missile launchers carrying a wide assortment of firepower from incendiary to fragmentation warheads. Among them were scattered APCs, no longer equipped with their standard anti-personnel, turret-mounted weapons, but rather with oversized cannons resembling a naval vessel's CIWS system. Each of the cannons could throw out a virtual *wall* high-powered rounds with a rate of fire that impressed even General Ston.

Though there were over three hundred infantrymen present, they were support for the vehicles and nothing more. General Ston had learned the hard way how ineffective infantry was against the Kaiju and there was no point in merely throwing more bodies onto the fire.

The tanks would be firing depleted uranium tipped shells and other munitions specifically designed to punch through whatever they were fired at. Some Kaiju had literal armor in place of flesh while others had exoskeletons similar to those of insect. It was these types of Kaiju that were the toughest to kill. Those whose flesh was merely flesh should fall quickly, he hoped.

The best estimate intel could give him placed the Kaiju still an hour out from landfall. The waiting for the great beasts to arrive would be the hardest part of the evening. Time like that allowed fear to grow and fester inside a man. Once the Kaiju actually showed themselves, one would be so busy trying to stay alive that fear no longer truly factored into the equation. Training took over and you either got the job done or you went home in a box.

Admiral Worley had promised heavy air support for his troops and General Ston was counting on it. His command was dug in. They would either hold this beach or die trying.

The sun was setting over the ocean. As its last rays reflected across the surface of the water, General Ston watched the enormous lights he had shipped in begin to be turned on. There were rows after row of them as well. The tanks and launchers didn't truly need them, but they bought an ease to the situation. A soldier who could see his enemy with his own eyes felt more secure than one relying solely on his instruments. At least that was the general's reasoning for the light placements.

An advanced model APC awaited the general. It, too, was equipped with the new "anti-Kaiju" cannon on its turret but that was far from the only upgrade to its overall systems. Most of its internal space was converted to house the gear that one would normally find in a mobile command unit. Large satellite dishes and other devices protruded from its roof locking its cannon into only a 180-degree axis instead of the 360 it otherwise would have had. It was a small price to pay however for all that was gained in the tradeoff.

Only Colonel Markham, who was a certified tech in numerous areas, and the APC's driver, Private Steward accompanied the general and he was fine with that. This was the most "hands on" he had been in over a decade and the thrill of it made him feel young again. When the battle began, General Ston would be directly linked into the combat net and able to not only see everything, up close and personal as it unfolded but also to relay orders to his men on the spot.

"It's almost time, sir," Colonel Markham informed him. "It would be best if we got inside now."

General Ston lowered the binoculars he'd been looking through and nodded.

"Carpe noctem, boys," he said towards his troops on the beach then turned to follow the colonel into the APC.

****

The Kaiju came. The waters of the ocean churned and foamed as the great beasts rose. The lead creature resembled something akin to an ant. Six legs moved under the fat orb of its body. Its head sat at the top of an elongated neck, much like a giraffe. Behind it was a Kaiju that stood on two legs like a man with the horns of a ram curled on the sides of its head. It lumbered forward, arms swaying as it moved. Still more Kaiju followed. The ground itself shook from the approach of the monsters. One of the Kaiju that was covered in a mix of wet fur and scales, charged ahead of the others. Its yellow slanted eyes blazed as it snarled, showing rows of razor teeth.

"All units, pick your targets and fire!" General Ston's voice cried over the combat net.

The first row of tanks let loose in a coordinated blast followed only a fraction of a second later by the row behind them. The cat Kaiju died almost instantly as the firepower that combined firepower of over sixty tanks slammed into it. The barrage of depleted uranium tipped shells thundered into it, shredding its flesh and punching holes in its chest, throat, and legs. Its massive body staggered backwards before splashing over to be covered by the waves.

The ant Kaiju skittered forward. The tanks fired again, but this time, the results were greatly different. Though some rounds cracked the thing's exoskeleton, most of them exploded on impact with no real penetration. The rows of tanks continued fire as the creature closed in on them. It waded into the first row, stabbing the sharpened points of its spear like feet through several of the tanks. The ant Kaiju began a dance of death upon the tanks. The main guns of those closest to it pivoted to come to bear upon the Kaiju, some firing at near point blank range as the ram Kaiju loped onto the shore. It approached an undamaged section of the front line and bent over to scoop up a tank in one of its hands. Its fingers closed around the vehicle, crushing it in its hand.

A fourth Kaiju emerged from the water and bounded on the beach. Though it had the body and legs of a man, it had no arms. They were replaced by masses of tentacles that whipped about in the air with a savage fury. At the end of each tentacle was a jagged pincer. The tentacled abomination tore into the tanks with a zealous glee. High-pitched squeals pierced the night from the three mouths that rested below a matching set of three, large black eyes.

At that moment, the air support General Ston had been promised arrived. Five full squadrons of F-16s came barreling in on the Kaiju. Missiles launched from their wings, filling the sky, as they blazed their way into the three Kaiju attacking the rows of tanks. The ones striking the ant Kaiju detonated against its exoskeleton with little effect beyond creating numerous flashes of light and heat across the length of its body. The ram Kaiju however staggered under the onslaught of missiles as their explosions blew chunks of flesh and bone into the air. The last of the three Kaiju already ashore brought up its tentacles, intercepting most of the missiles before they could make contact with its body. Though it lost some pincers and limbs to the volley of fire, it stood its ground.

Seeing a chance to finish one of the Kaiju, General Ston ordered the mobile missile launchers behind the rows of the tanks to target the ram Kaiju. Half a dozen of them opened up on it, getting the job done. A lucky shot from one of the launchers reduced the ram Kaiju's head to a mess of bloody pulp that rained over the sand of the beach.

Four more Kaiju had risen from the waves. The F-16s found themselves flying directly toward these new monsters. They split up, breaking their formations, in order to present less of a target to the Kaiju. One of the monsters resembled a dragon straight out of myth except for the fact that it had Godzilla like legs. Huge wings unfolded from its back as its jaws parted and jagged bolts of electrical energy erupted to tear into the F-16s. In a flash similar to striking chain lightning, nine of the F-16s blew to pieces as the energy crackled, arcing from one plane to another. The dragon Kaiju took flight, giving chase, as the remaining F-16s punched it and their afterburners blazed blue.

General Ston slammed a fist into the console below the screen where he watched the battle from inside the highly modified APC that served as his command post. Odds were that it was the last he would be seeing of his air support.

Of the other three new Kaiju, the most disturbing was the one that led the others ashore. It towered over four hundred feet tall. The creature had four arms, two of each side of its body. It had no hands, however. Each arm ended in an open, rounded stump. Blue fire swirled inside them as the Kaiju aimed them at the rows of tanks. Streams of fire erupted from them, spraying over the shore's defenders, melting the armor of the tanks and turning the sand under them to glass.

"Take that thing out now!" General Ston ordered the reserve missile launchers.

Half of the remaining launcher still carrying unfired payloads spat death at the creature. Missile after missile poured into the monster. One blast tore an arm from the thing's body. Another ripped a charred groove across its side. As the creature brought up one of its stumps to target the incoming volleys, a missile disappeared into the stump's opening. The explosion dwarfed those of the other missiles making contact with the Kaiju as the stump disintegrated in a blast of blue that lit up the entire beach. The four-armed monster toppled to the sand, as a crack, emitting more of the same blue energy, rippled across its body, and then went dark. The Kaiju did not get back to its feet. It lay still, its corpse smoking on the sand.

There was little left of the two rows of tanks. Their crews were diving out of them as the vehicles were too dug in to flee themselves effectively. General Ston slumped in his seat aboard the command unit. The battle had been decided in a matter of minutes. He knew the remaining missile launchers didn't have enough firepower left to stop the Kaiju.

He was about to give the order to fallback as his phone began to ring. He jerked his cell from his pocket and flipped it open. "General Ston," he answered.

"General," Admiral Hutchinson said. "You have to hold on for a few more minutes. Dr. Bryson and his bio-weapon are en route. Do you understand me?"

Ston wanted to reached through the phone and strangle the navy officer. "Hold?" He growled the word. "Hold with what?"

"I don't know," Admiral Hutchinson said, "but do it!"

General Ston heard the admiral end the call. "Damn you," he raged. "Damn you to hell!"

His anger vented, he refocused his attention on the battle. There were nine of the Kaiju on the beach now and his tanks were gone. The few units still operational according to his board had been abandoned by their crews who were now running up the beach in utter terror.

"All remaining batteries, target the Kaiju, and hit those bastards with everything you got!"

Even as the launchers emptied their last missiles, General Ston's eyes raked over the screen, searching for other ways to buy time. Most of the APCS tasked as support were operational. Ordering them to stand alone against the Kaiju would be sentencing their crews to death but there was no other choice. Sometimes in war sacrifices had to be made. He gave the order for them to stand fast and then shouted at his driver and Colonel Markham. "Take us in!"

"Sir?" Colonel Markham stared at him.

"You heard me," Ston yelled at the colonel so violently that spittle flew from his lips with the words. "We have to buy some time or we've lost a lot more than just this battle!"

"Yes sir," the command unit's driver reluctantly acknowledged the order.

The command unit's mounted CIWS like weapon chattered, hosing the closest of the Kaiju with a virtual wall of high-powered rounds as the vehicle sprang forward towards the monster.

****

Dr. Jerry Bryson stood in the rear compartment of the lead bomber, making last second adjustments to the airburst cylinder containing the virus he and his team had created.

"Time's up, Dr. Bryson!" one of the bomber's crew yelled at him. "We need to clear this area now!"

Jerry had been around military personnel long enough in the last week or so to know better than to try to argue with the soldier. He followed the man out of the bay. Thick airlock doors clanged shut behind them as they exited.

The bomber Jerry was aboard was only one of four that

carried airburst cylinders of the virus. In the moments to come, all four would be dropping the cylinders above the mass of Kaiju below. Jerry's worst nightmares about the virus played through his mind as he entered the bomber's cockpit and took a seat behind its pilots. *If* the virus worked at all, only the Lord himself knew what sort of effect it would have on the monsters. It was designed to kill them as it attached itself to the Kaiju's DNA and eat them from the inside out like a fast acting cancer. Anyhow, that was what it was *designed* to do but Jerry and his team had never gotten the chance to test it properly on a full scale, live Kaiju. There was nothing he could do at this point though other than wait and pray.

The quartet of bombers flew over the Kaiju as their bay doors opened and the cylinders fell earthward. The four cylinders burst apart as they fell, releasing clouds of gas that filled the air and turned the glow of the shoreline's giant searchlight emplacements an eerie shade of green.

Almost instantly, the Kaiju began to screech and wail as the gas made contact with them. Their cries could be heard even inside the bomber over the loud roar of its engines as its pilot struggled to take it higher, outside of the Kaiju's counterattack range.

****

The mobile command APC jarred to a halt as its driver slammed on its brakes at General Ston's order. The General raced to its topside hatch and climbed up into its turret. The night air stunk like rotten eggs. Ston figured he must be breathing in the virus Dr. Bryson had designed and hoped it wasn't harmful to humans. Not far from the APC's position, a Kaiju, shaped like a great, bipedal lizard came staggering towards it. It didn't take a genius to see that the monster was hurting. Its skin bubbled as rivers of purple pus poured from the growing ulcers that covered the thing's body.

The Kaiju in front of General Ston's mobile command unit

collapsed to one knee. More purple ooze leaked from the corners of its mouth as it roared in pain once more. Similar scenes were playing out all over the beach, as one by one, the great beasts toppled over to sprawl out onto the sand. Cheers rang out from the fleeing tank crews and scattered infantry troopers who were still alive.

"That bastard did it," General Ston muttered then said more loudly, "He really did it!"

Some of the Kaiju appeared more resistant than others were, but even those who didn't die outright from exposure to the clouds of the virus carried by the night wind appeared greatly weakened by it.

General Ston cheered himself as over four dozen Apaches and Cobras flew overhead, opening fire on the surviving Kaiju. The tide of the battle had turned in an instant and suddenly it was the Kaiju who were on the run.

One Kaiju, shaped like a giant crab, waddled towards the ocean. Its movements were awkward and labored. Missiles and the blazing cannons of several Apaches tore into the monster, knocking it over. It rolled on the beach, legs frantically slashing about, as the thing tried to right itself and failed.

Its shell fractured and broke apart as more missiles hammered into its struggling form.

Another Kaiju with entire sections of its skeleton exposed from where Dr. Bryson's virus had eaten away its flesh sprinted for the water. It dove into the ocean, vanishing from sight as General Ston raised his fist upwards toward the sky. He gave a victory shout as the last of the Kaiju either fell or fled.

****

Hours later, General Ston, Colonel Markham, and Dr. Bryson stood side by side atop a hill overlooking the beach. As far as the eye could see, the sands were covered with the bodies of dead men and Kaiju alike. Tendrils of smoke still rose toward the heavens from the rows of crumpled and burnt out husks of tanks.

"This is going to be hell to clean up," Colonel Markham said to no one in particular.

General Ston and Jerry ignored him. They were lost in their own conversation.

"Guess I owe you an apology, son," the general admitted. "I didn't think you'd be able to come through in time."

"No apology needed, General," Jerry said. "And you shouldn't be thanking me just yet."

"Doctor, you've just given us a means to fight back the Kaiju wherever they show up." The General waved a hand at the beach. "And it sure won't come at anywhere near as high a price as stopping them here did."

"Not counting any that haven't been discovered in the water yet, there are eleven dead Kaiju down there, Doctor Bryson," Colonel Markham punched Jerry in the shoulder. "And we didn't have to resort to nuking our own land like the Russians did in order to achieve that."

"Colonel Markham is right, Dr. Bryson," General Ston smiled. "Whether you like it or not, you're a hero."

"There are a lot more Kaiju out there," Jerry told them instead of saying what he was really thinking. *We've just released a manmade, completely untested, biological weapon into the atmosphere and there's no way to know what the long term effects of that are going to mean for us. Only time is going to tell us that.*

"Cheer up, doc," Colonel Markham laughed. "Being a hero ain't so bad. You might even get a medal out of this."

"Oh, you can bet that I'll see that he does." General Ston grinned like a feral cat examining its prey as he met Jerry's eyes.

****

Sarge Hooper led a group of soldiers along the beach. An open transport truck in reverse carefully kept pace with them. Hooper's squad was one of many tasked with collecting and cataloging the bodies of the dead in the wake of the battle. It was gruesome and tiring work but just another day in the army to Hooper. He was a career grunt and content with his lot in life.

The transport truck was half-full and less than a hour had passed. There was just so many of the dead. The ones in pieces and those that were little more than squashed masses of broken bone were the worst. They weren't as easily moved as the more intact corpses and Hooper hated dealing with them. Some were so badly pulped they had to be loaded onto the truck with shovels.

Dried blood and other bodily fluids caked Hooper's uniform and the gloves covering his hands. The body on the sand in front of him was intact for the most part. The soldier looked to have been not much more than a kid. One of those gung-ho, redneck types who enlisted to kick some butt, Hooper wagered. Friendly fire had taken him out. There were two gaping holes in the kid, one in his chest that Hooper could have fitted this fist through if he had been inclined to do so and another in his stomach. The smell the of strands of ruptured intestines, oozing crap and poking out of the kid's gut wound, made Hooper gag. The biohazard mask he wore didn't always filter the odor of the corpses. Some were just so strong they got into the mask no matter what.

Hooper thought about calling Burt or Eddie over to deal with the kid but opted not to. He hated COs who did things like that and swore he wasn't going to be one of them. Hooper manned up and bent over to get hold of the kid's body. As he did so, the kid opened his eyes.

"Holy…!" Hooper screamed, almost tripping over another corpse, as he backed away from the kid. *How in the hell is this kid still alive?* He wondered, as the young soldier began to stir and a low moan rose from the kid's throat.

"We got a live one!" Hooper barked at Burt who was the closet member of his squad. "Call a medic over here!"

Hooper's attention was focused on Burt. He didn't see the young soldier leap up from the sand and come at him until the kid's hands were on him. Hooper felt the cold of the kid's fingers through his uniform as they closed on his shoulders and jerked him around. He stared into the glazed over, vacant eyes of the young soldier in utter disbelief as the kid pulled him closer still. The kid's teeth clamped shut on Hooper's nose, biting it off his face. Blood flew as Hooper yelped and shoved the kid away from him. The kid stumbled and fell back to the sand, chewing on the hunk of Hooper's nose in his mouth.

One of Hooper's hands rose to apply pressure to what was left of his nose on his face as one of his heavy combat boots lashed out at the kid. It smashed into the young soldier with jarring force. The kid moaned again, ignoring the blow, and started to get back to his feet.

"Frag this!" Hooper drew his sidearm and put a round into the young soldier's forehead. Brain matter sprayed out from the exit wound that the bullet blew in the backside of the kid's skull.

"What the hell?" Burt shouted, already rushing over to where Hooper stood.

"Bit my freaking nose off," Hooper snapped through the blood that poured down into his mouth as he spoke.

"What?" Burt asked as Hooper realized his words were coming out mangled and distorted because of the missing part of his nose.

"Hey!" Burt said excitedly as more of the bodies around them began to move. "More of these guys are alive."

Hooper shook his head, flinging droplets of red that leaked through the fingers of his hand covering the mess of his face. He gestured violently at the young soldier's body and then at his wound.

"You really need to get that looked at, Sarge," Burt said, "That's pretty bad, man."

Hooper's eyes widened as the twitching forms of the other dead soldiers around them began to get to their feet. Burt remained oblivious to the danger around them. Hooper took aim at another of the soldiers.

"Sarge! What's wrong with you?" Burt cried out, rushing him in attempt to knock the pistol from his hand.

Sporadic gunfire rang out from other areas of the beach as Hooper shoved Burt away from him.

The dead surrounding them sprang forward. Hooper managed to swing his pistol back around. It cracked, muzzle flashing orange, as he put a round into the chest of a soldier who was missing most of his face. Its right side was a slagged mess of charred flesh. The bullet caused the dead soldier to stumble, but it didn't stop him.

Burt was screaming. Hooper glanced over his shoulder and saw three of the dead soldiers holding Burt. Their teeth were ripping chunks of flesh from his shoulders and arms. Hooper had no time to help the private, because more of the dead soldiers were closing in on him. Hooper squeezed the trigger of his pistol three more times, firing into the mass of dead men, before he broke and ran.

****

"What in the Hades?" General Ston blurted out as he, Colonel Markham, and Jerry heard the gunfire from the beach. It had started out with a few shots here and there, and it had grown to a crescendo that sounded like a full out battle taking place.

From their spot atop the hill, they could see soldiers firing on other soldiers. Those who weren't firing were either locked in hand to hand to combat against each other or running for their lives.

"Colonel?" General Ston asked.

"No idea, sir," Markham answered, "but I am on it."

The colonel raced towards the mobile command unit and the comm system inside it.

Jerry noticed a group of soldiers climbing up the hill. There was something off about how they were moving.

"General," Jerry said.

General Ston turned to him.

"I think it'd be best if we followed the colonel."

"What's that?" General Ston paused as if trying to hear something over the sound of the gunfire. "Are those men...moaning?"

The group of soldiers moving up the hill was only a few dozen yards away now. Jerry saw that one of them was missing an arm. Another limped along on an oddly bent leg that appeared to be badly broken. The white of bone poked through the dried blood-caked cloth of his torn pants.

Jerry became lost in the fight or flight of the adrenaline that was coursing through his veins. He grabbed the general by the arm and yanked him into movement. The two of them ran for the mobile command unit. Jerry slid the heavy side door of the vehicle closed behind them once they were inside.

Colonel Markham sat in the chair at the comm console. "General, I've got reports coming in from all over of the wounded attacking those trying to help them!"

"What is this?" General Ston demanded of Jerry. "Some kind of mass hysteria or something?"

"I'm not *that* kind of doctor," Jerry snapped at him. "It could be a side effect of the virus. I told you it was untested."

"Uh, sir..." Private Steward called through the open door leading to the driver's compartment. "We've got company!"

Jerry and the general hurried to stand behind Private Steward, staring out the command unit's forward window. Dozens of soldiers were advancing on the vehicle. The general squinted, getting as good a look at the men outside as he could given the distance still between them and the command unit.

"Those men aren't wounded. They're dead, aren't they, Dr. Bryson?"

Jerry frowned. "Yes, I think they are."

General Ston grabbed Jerry by the front of his shirt and slammed him into the wall of the driver's compartment. "Your virus did this, didn't it?"

"I don't know," Jerry cried. "Maybe"

"You little fragger," General Ston said and drew his sidearm. Jerry struggled, fighting back, as the general pressed its barrel painfully into Jerry's forehead. The metal of the barrel cut into his flesh as Ston used the barrel to hold Jerry's head in place against the wall. The last thing Jerry heard was a popping noise as the pistol fired and then there was only darkness.

****

Amid the chaos on the beach, no one noticed as the antenna of the ant Kaiju began to twitch and flick about. Huge holes spotted the thing's corpse, its inside spilling out from them, as it began to stand up.

Epilogue

Admiral Hutchinson had been rushed to the bunker buried under the mountains of Colorado. The President was dead. A winged Kaiju had overtaken Air Force One en route and taken the plane apart with its beak. The last anyone had seen of Air Force One was a satellite image of the winged Kaiju picking through its wreckage. The dead Kaiju were even more dangerous than the live ones. Like their dead human counterparts, they too hungered for the flesh of the living.

On the upside, their hunger wasn't limited to live human flesh. They hunted the surviving living Kaiju as well. During his own flight to the bunker, the admiral had witnessed a clash between two of the titans. A living beast that reminded him of something from a Godzilla film had been locked in lethal combat with another that resembled a cross between a giant dog and fish. The dogfish thing's body was covered in ulcers that bled slime like purplish goo and it was clearly dead. However, that didn't stop it from going after the lizard-like one in a hunger driven rage.

The admiral sat alone in the room he'd claimed as his office. A half empty bottle of vodka sat on his desk as he read over the latest batch of reports on the world outside. What little remained of the US military had concentrated in the middle portion of the country and were engaged fighting a desperate holding action against not only the Kaiju, who now had free rein of the land and oceans alike, but also the dead. The rest of America had been abandoned. The hungry dead outnumbered the living by somewhere close to five to one in the US now and things were only getting worse.

The vice president was a twit and incapable of making the hard calls that needed to be made so Admiral Hutchinson ordered him to be shot. Leadership of the entire remainder of the human race in America had fallen to Hutchinson in the process since General Ston had been lost in the initial outbreak of what most folks were calling "The Bryson Virus." It wasn't a position he wanted, but that didn't matter. Someone had to be in command if anyone was going to survive. It didn't help matters that many of those left alive blamed the military for causing the dead to rise up and turn on the living.

Admiral Hutchinson would have preferred to be leading those that remained from the US battle carrier group that had been ordered south to Antarctica. Neither the Kaiju nor the dead could deal with the cold very well and that was just about the only advantage the human race had at the moment. Sending the battle carrier and its fleet that far south would protect it, he hoped, because otherwise the oceans belonged to the Kaiju as much as the once great cities of man now belonged to the dead.

He reached for the bottle of vodka and stopped himself as his hands touched its glass surface. Tears welled up in his eyes as he released the bottle and buried his head in his hands. There was only so much one man could endure, he told himself. Maybe this was the end of the world. Maybe it wasn't, but either way, the future of humanity rested in his hands.

The End

www.ingramcontent.com/pod-product-compliance
Lightning Source LLC
Chambersburg PA
CBHW070650130626
46555CB00006B/2802